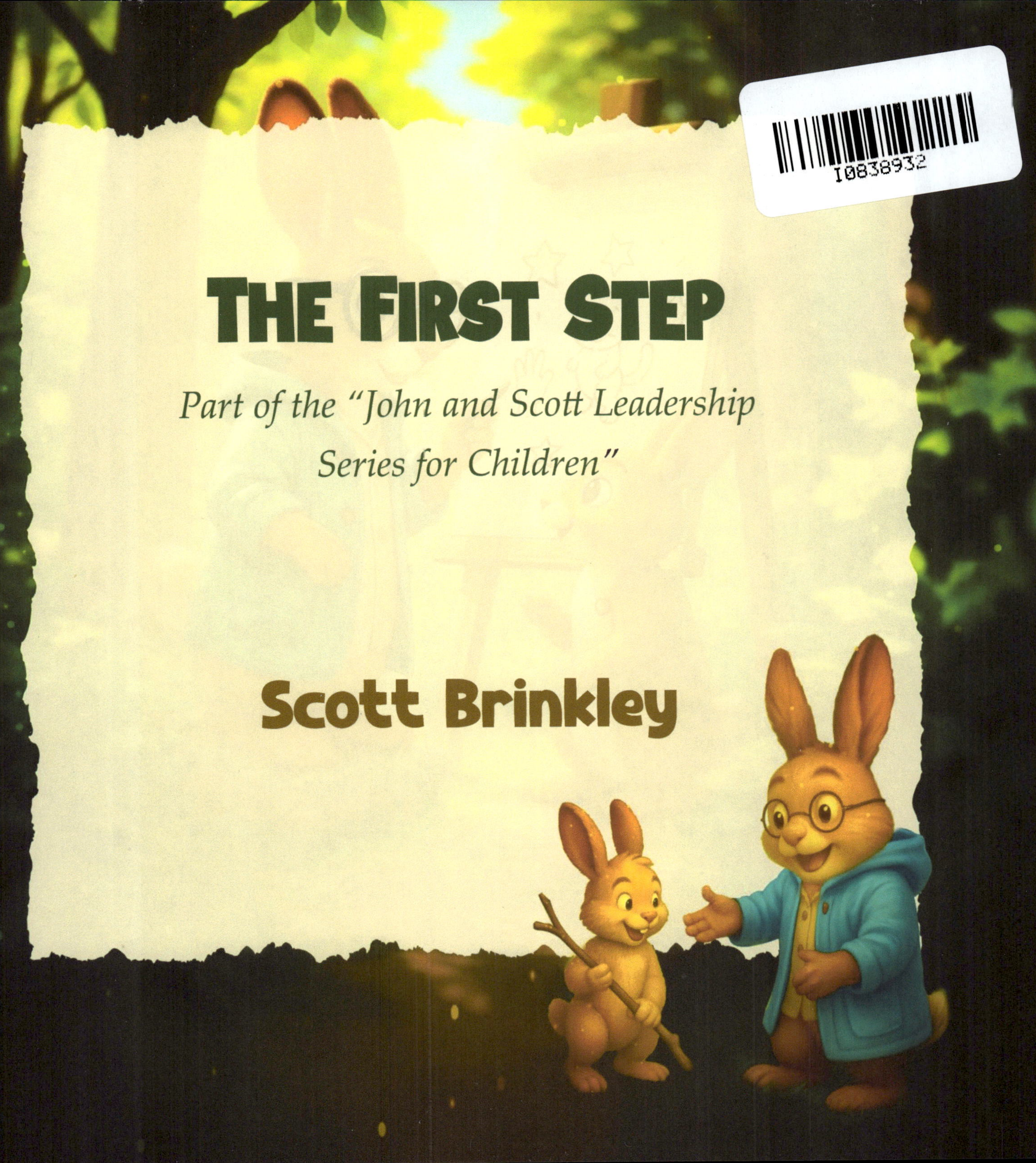

THE FIRST STEP
Part of the "John and Scott Leadership Series for Children"
Scott Brinkley

Copyright © 2025

All Rights Reserved

No part of this book may be reproduced, stored,
or shared in any way, whether electronic or mechanical,
without the written permission of the author.

Exceptions may apply only as permitted by law.

Dedication

As a serial entrepreneur, I have deep respect for those who take the leap into business. Entrepreneurs not only take risks for themselves, but also for every person they employ. I only wish I had learned earlier the life lessons I know today.

One day, I told my seven-year-old daughter, Reese. I'd pay her $100 for every book she reads after the age of ten. She lit up with excitement and asked, "Can I start now?"

I told her yes, but I would pick the books. When she asked why, I explained that there are certain things, that if you know them, they will make your life easier, but they require a bit more maturity to understand.

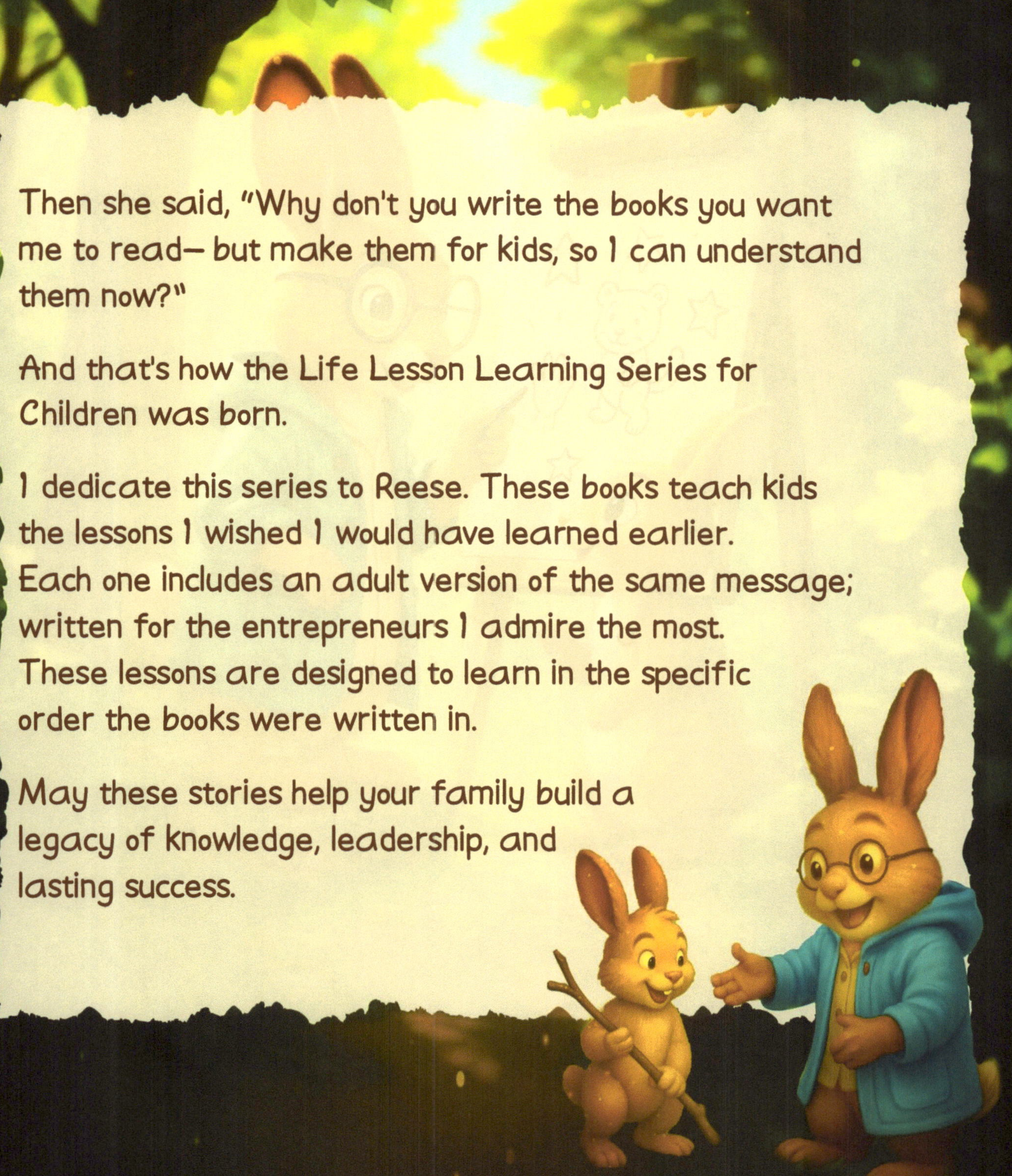

Then she said, "Why don't you write the books you want me to read— but make them for kids, so I can understand them now?"

And that's how the Life Lesson Learning Series for Children was born.

I dedicate this series to Reese. These books teach kids the lessons I wished I would have learned earlier. Each one includes an adult version of the same message; written for the entrepreneurs I admire the most. These lessons are designed to learn in the specific order the books were written in.

May these stories help your family build a legacy of knowledge, leadership, and lasting success.

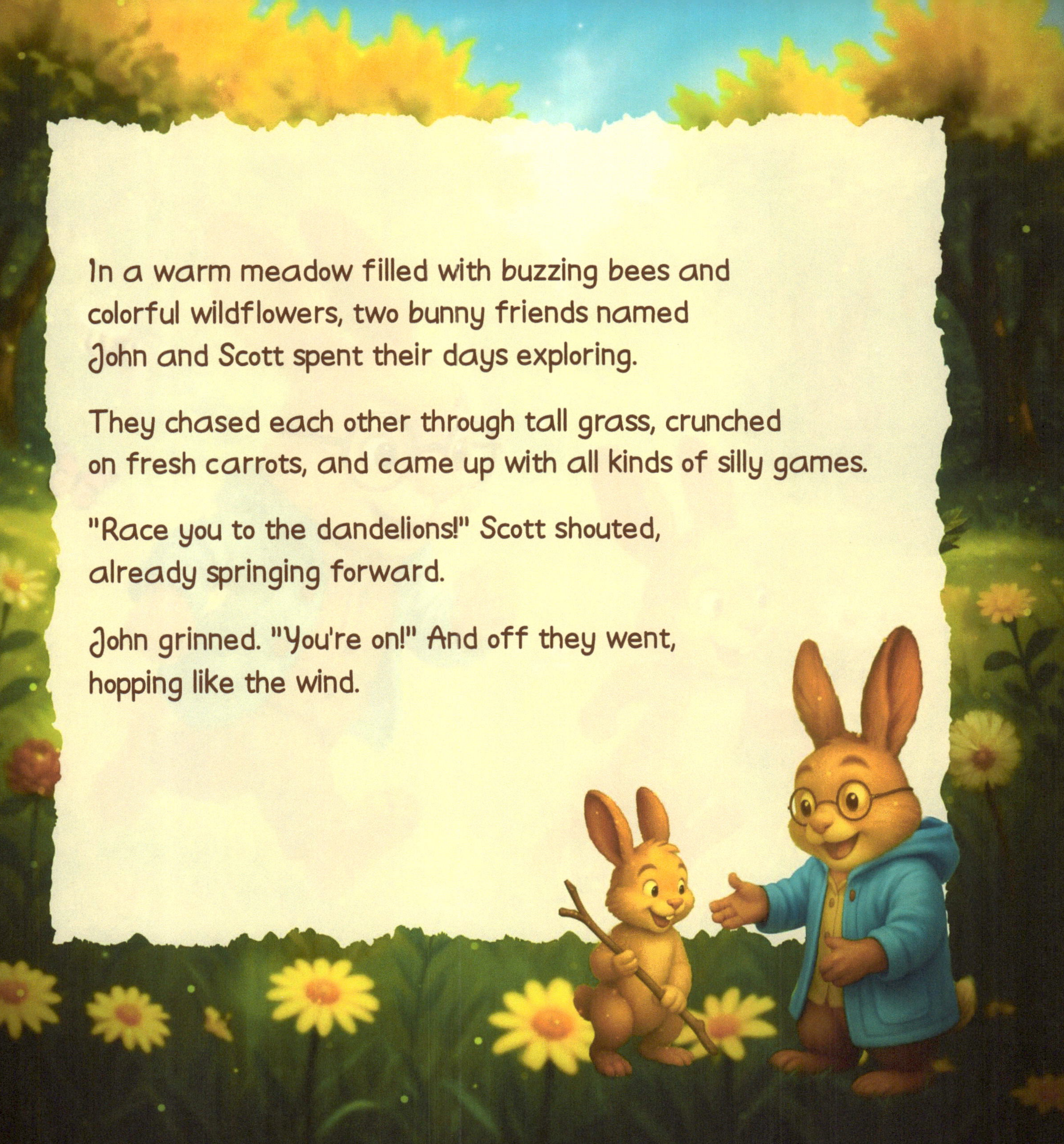

In a warm meadow filled with buzzing bees and colorful wildflowers, two bunny friends named John and Scott spent their days exploring.

They chased each other through tall grass, crunched on fresh carrots, and came up with all kinds of silly games.

"Race you to the dandelions!" Scott shouted, already springing forward.

John grinned. "You're on!" And off they went, hopping like the wind.

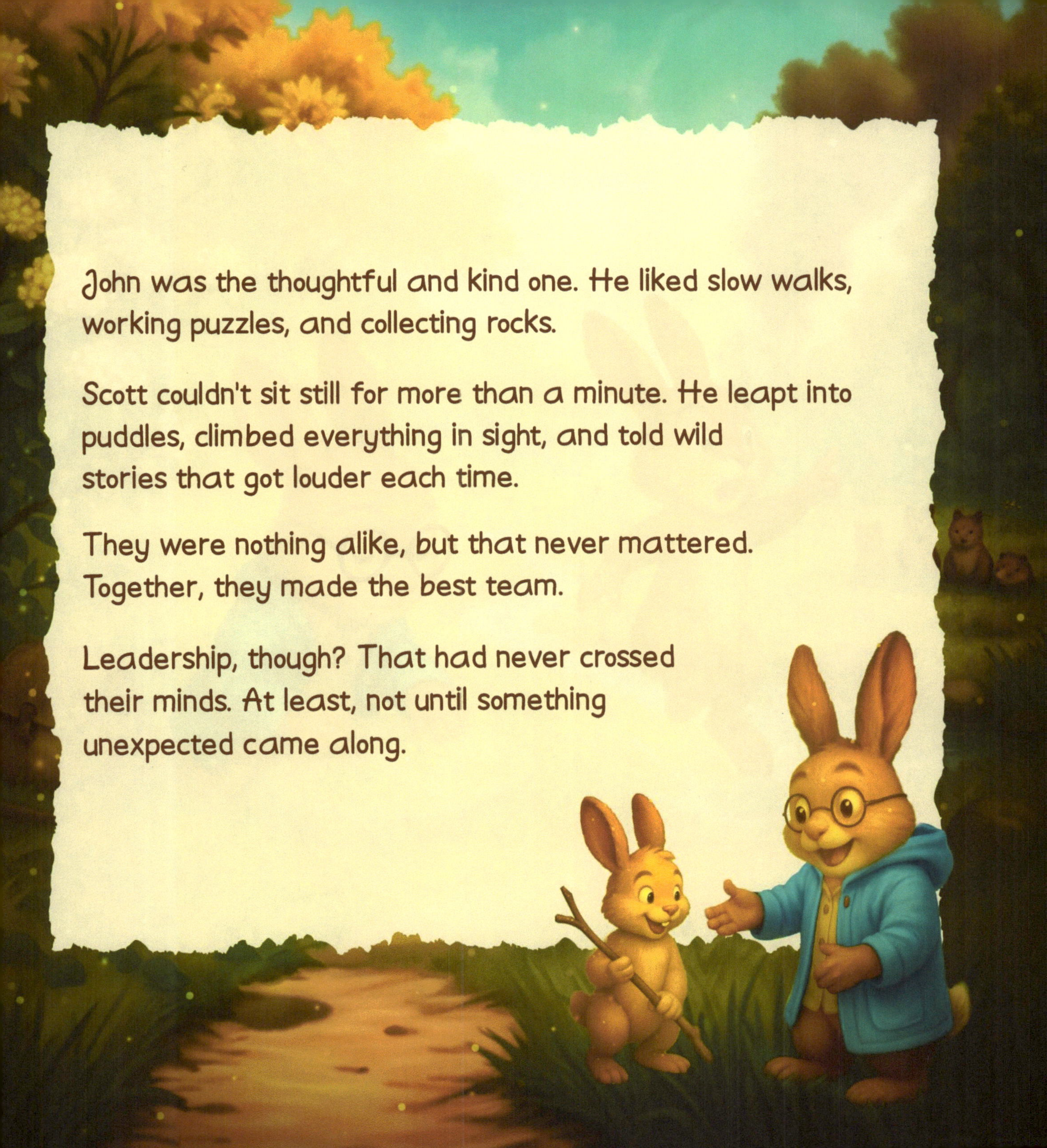

John was the thoughtful and kind one. He liked slow walks, working puzzles, and collecting rocks.

Scott couldn't sit still for more than a minute. He leapt into puddles, climbed everything in sight, and told wild stories that got louder each time.

They were nothing alike, but that never mattered. Together, they made the best team.

Leadership, though? That had never crossed their minds. At least, not until something unexpected came along.

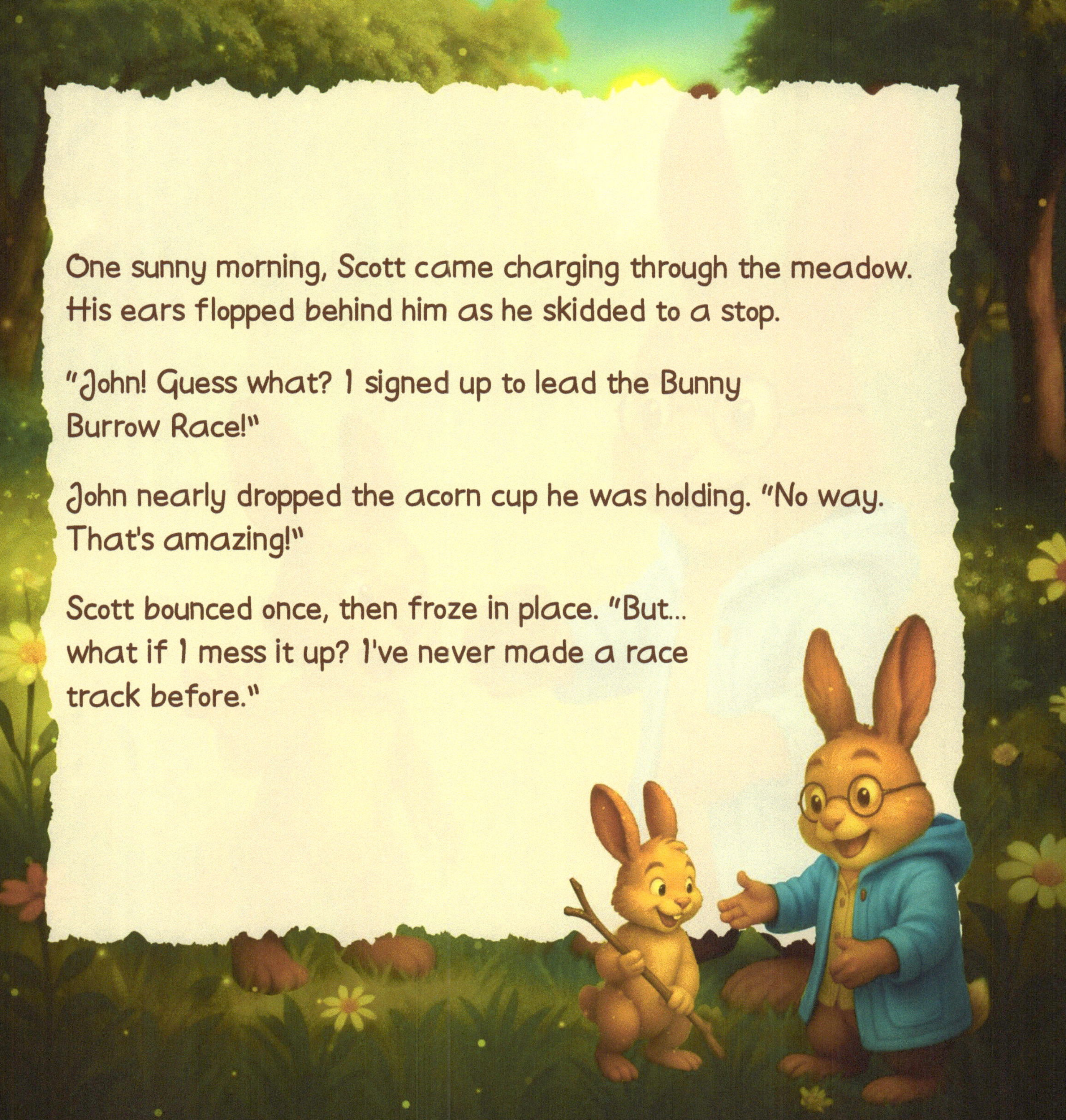

One sunny morning, Scott came charging through the meadow. His ears flopped behind him as he skidded to a stop.

"John! Guess what? I signed up to lead the Bunny Burrow Race!"

John nearly dropped the acorn cup he was holding. "No way. That's amazing!"

Scott bounced once, then froze in place. "But... what if I mess it up? I've never made a race track before."

Scott lowered his ears and stared at the ground.

"Maybe I shouldn't do it."

John looked puzzled.

"Why not?"

"Because leaders are supposed to know everything. And I don't," Scott said with a sigh.

John gave a little smile. "You don't need to know everything.

You just need to care enough to try.

You decided to build it, and I'll be right there to help you."

Scott's eyes lit up. "Really?"

"Of course. That's what friends do.

And honestly, that's what good leaders do too."

So they got to work. They picked out sticks to mark the course,
stacked small stones for jumping points, used giant
leaves for flags, and rolled an old basket into place for
the final tunnel.

Scott held up a crooked branch.

"Think this could work for the starting gate?"

John nodded. "Definitely. And we can wrap flowers
around it to make it look cool."

The more they worked, the more excited they
became and soon their ideas came
to life.

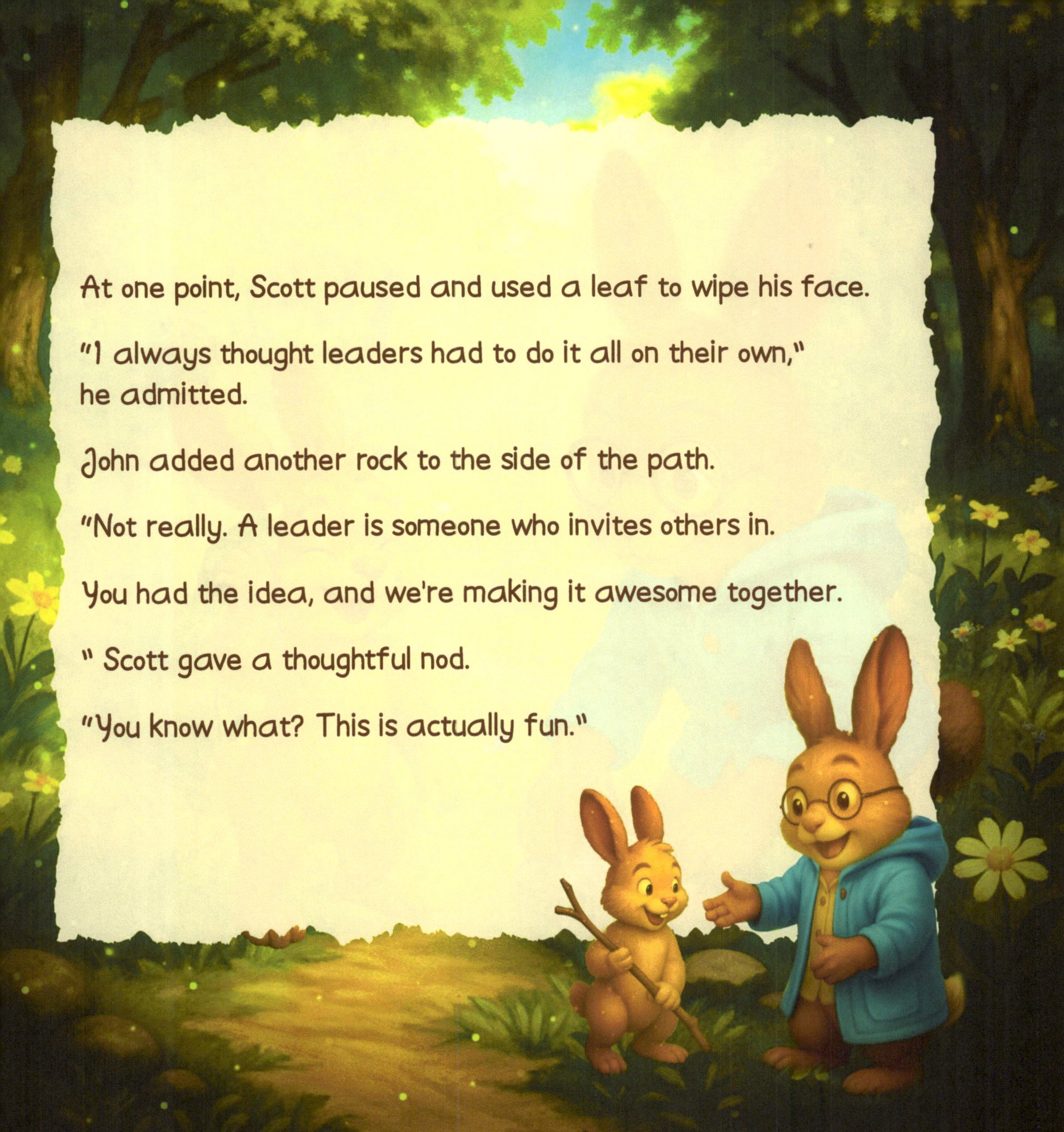

At one point, Scott paused and used a leaf to wipe his face.

"I always thought leaders had to do it all on their own,"
he admitted.

John added another rock to the side of the path.

"Not really. A leader is someone who invites others in.

You had the idea, and we're making it awesome together.

" Scott gave a thoughtful nod.

"You know what? This is actually fun."

Whoa

By the time the sun started to set,
the racecourse was finished.

There were jumps, twisty tunnels, slippery mud pits
(Scott insisted), and cheering corners (John's suggestion).

Scott stood back and looked at the whole thing.

His eyes were wide with wonder.

"Whoa. We really made this."

John gave him a big smile.

"Tomorrow's going to be great."

Scott leaned closer. "Thanks for helping me."

"Always," John replied.

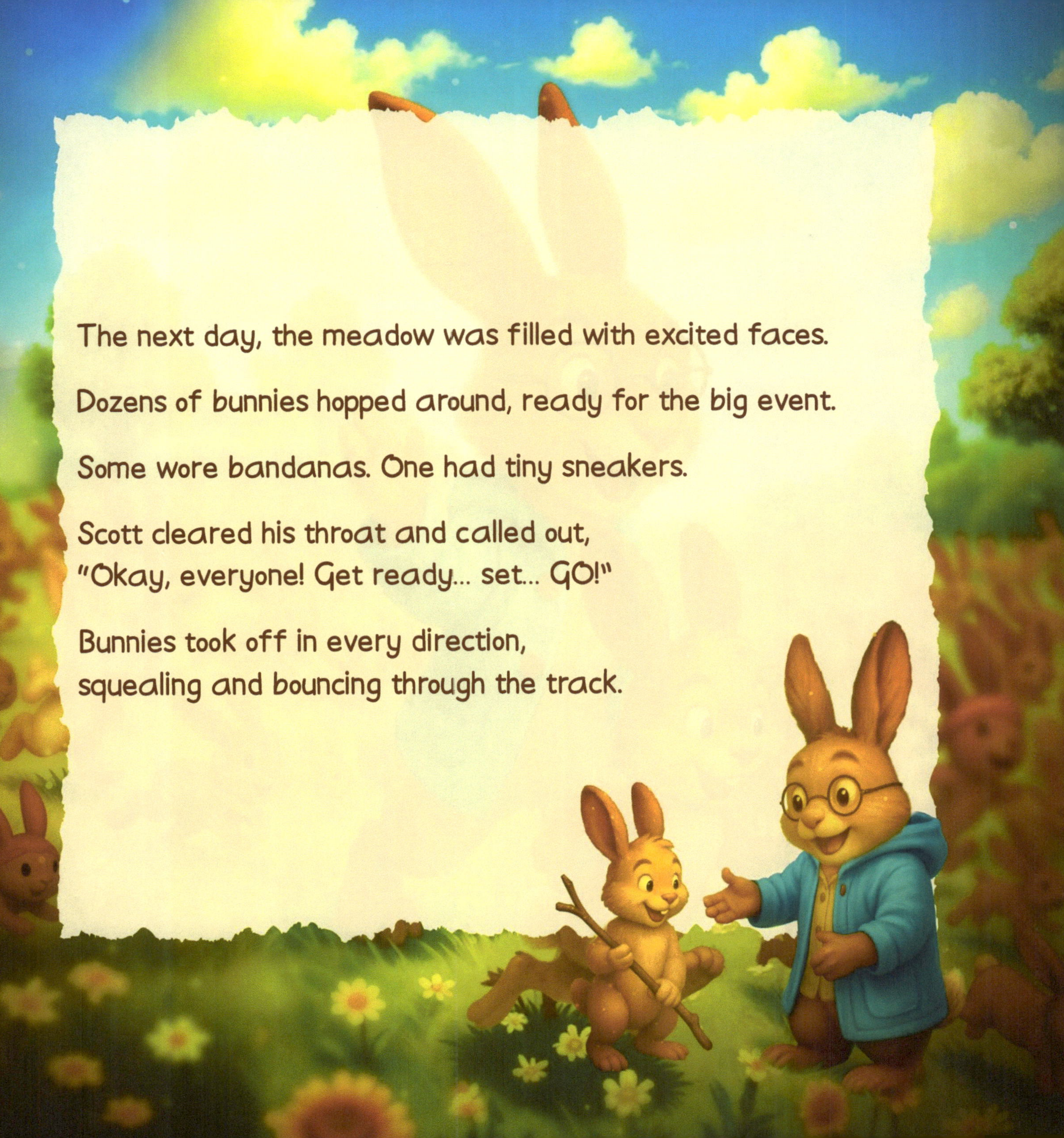

The next day, the meadow was filled with excited faces.

Dozens of bunnies hopped around, ready for the big event.

Some wore bandanas. One had tiny sneakers.

Scott cleared his throat and called out,
"Okay, everyone! Get ready... set... GO!"

Bunnies took off in every direction,
squealing and bouncing through the track.

There were tumbles, giggles, flying leaves, and loud cheering.

One bunny got stuck in the tunnel and wiggled out laughing.

John waved a flag from the side, while

Scott handed out carrot slices to tired racers.

Even the quietest bunnies joined in. Scott looked around at the happy crowd. His face lit up with joy.

"This feels like something magical," he said.

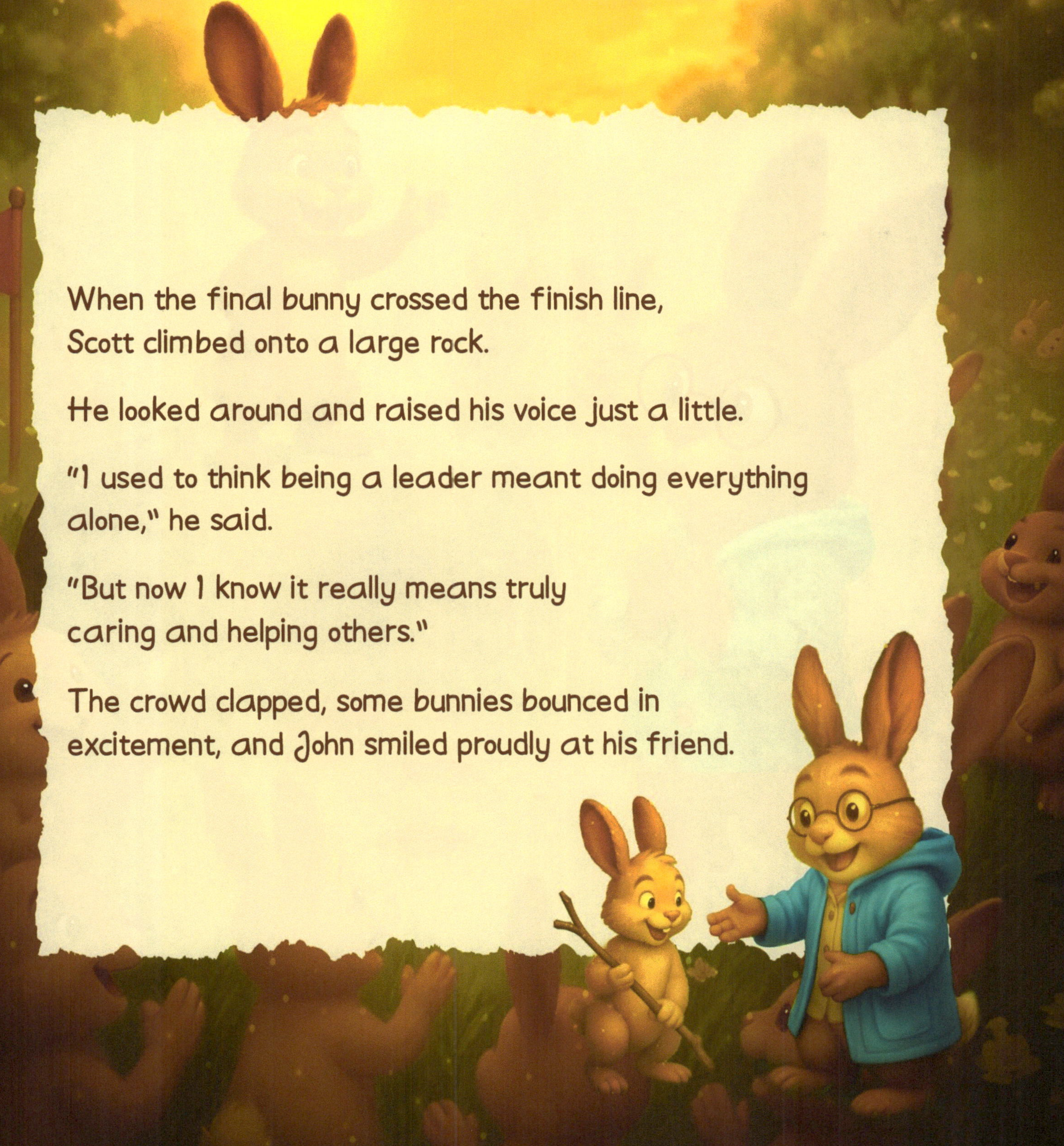

When the final bunny crossed the finish line,
Scott climbed onto a large rock.

He looked around and raised his voice just a little.

"I used to think being a leader meant doing everything
alone," he said.

"But now I know it really means truly
caring and helping others."

The crowd clapped, some bunnies bounced in
excitement, and John smiled proudly at his friend.

That night, under a sky full of stars, John and
Scott lay on their backs in the grass.

Their fur was messy, and their paws were tired,
but their hearts felt warm and full.

"I'm glad you didn't quit," John said.

Scott let out a long yawn.

"Me too. I think we both showed what leadership
looks like today."

The two stared quietly at the moon, feeling the
bond getting stronger than ever.

The two little bunnies had taken their first important step.

They were not just into leading others, but had found courage, kindness, and a friendship that would grow for the rest of their lives.

The Lesson

By the age of 35, I had built and sold multiple businesses before I learned one of the most important lessons of my life.

Most of my decisions were made with one question in mind: What's in it for me?

Sure, I had helped people along the way and even changed some lives— but it wasn't intentional.

My focus was on my own success and that of my family.

Then everything changed.

I made a conscious decision to help others get what
they want— and to make that my number one mission.

I found joy in watching others grow, succeed, and thrive.

I was energized by their wins: new homes,
career promotions, financial breakthroughs.

And for the first time, I was doing it all on purpose,
with no expectation of anything in return.

That's when I discovered the power of reciprocity.

When you genuinely help people, they often feel
compelled to help you back. I had unknowingly built
a reserve in what I now call the
"Reciprocity Help Bank."

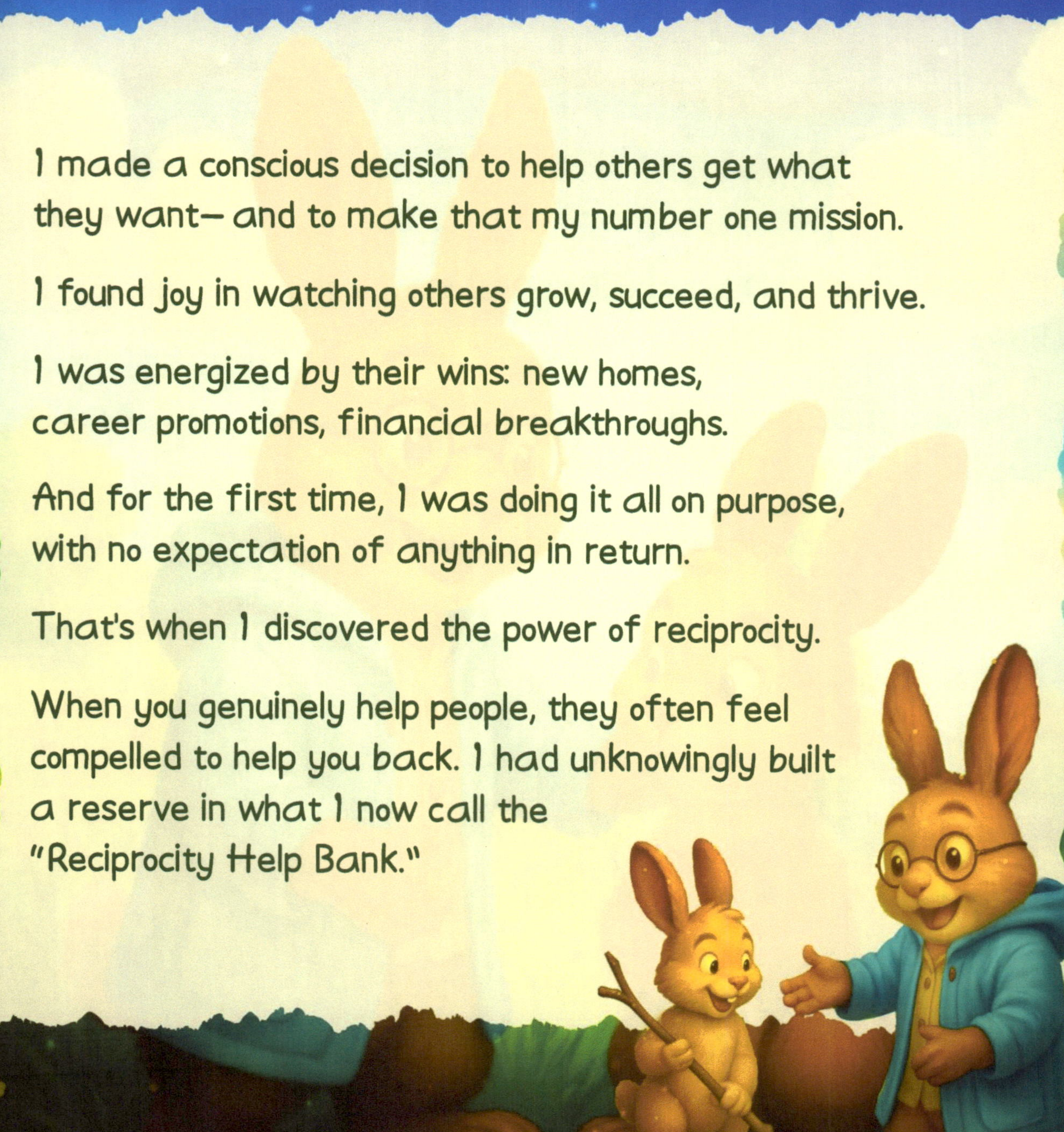

And when I need support, the return on that investment
was greater than I could've imagined.

Now, at 53, I've had the honor of working alongside
thousands of business owners in the home services industry.

I'm humbled and grateful for this lesson—
but I only wish I had learned it at age 8.

My hope is this book helps you grow as an
entrepreneur and pass this lesson on to kids.

If they make helping others their mission early in
life, I can say with full confidence: they'll live
a richer, more fulfilling life.

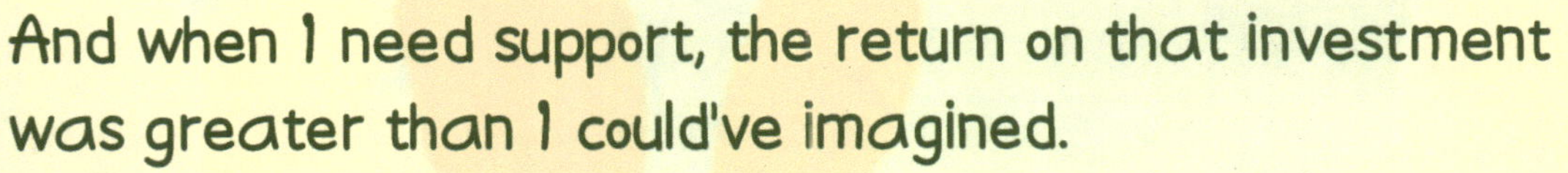

www.ingramcontent.com/pod-product-compliance
Lightning Source LLC
Chambersburg PA
CBHW041414300726
48978CB00002B/88